NOAH'S GARDEN

When Someone You Love Is in the Hospital

Mo Johnson   illustrated by Annabelle Josse

CANDLEWICK PRESS

Noah is flying
in seaplanes again—
silver seaplanes.

They lift and they zoom
and they loop in the sky.

"Hellooooo."
Grandad waves.

Noah gets dizzy and lands.
Seaplanes fly gracefully in Noah's garden.

Noah is bathing with tigers again.
Soapy tigers.
They splash and they flap
and they splosh in the pool.

"Look there," Grandad says, pointing.
Up floats a bubble. It pops.

Tigers wash cheerfully in Noah's garden.

"When can Jessica
  come to my garden?" Noah asks.

"Maybe someday soon," says Dad,
  spinning him around.

"Maybe next week," says Mom.
"Will you push her stroller?"

Noah nods.
There are lots of strollers
in Noah's garden.

But there's no baby Jessica.

Noah is riding on camels again.
Crazy camels.

They flop and they thump
and they flump through the sand.

"Ouch! Ouch!" cries Noah.

"They're too bumpy," says Gran.

Camels run clumsily
in Noah's garden.

Noah is dancing with penguins again.
Bouncing penguins.

They dip and they flip
and they bump on the ice.

"Watch me!" squeals Noah.
His feet tap the beat.

Penguins bop happily in Noah's garden.

"Please can Jessica play in my garden?"

"Maybe someday soon," says Dad,
  lifting Noah high.

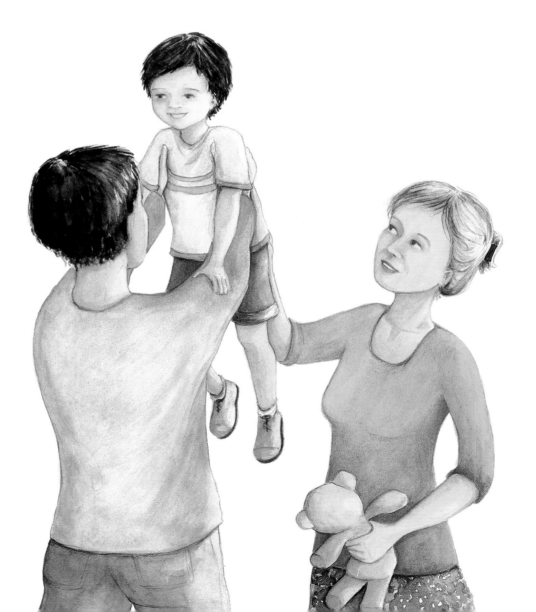

"Maybe next week," says Mom.
"She's with her doctor now."

Noah scowls.
There are always doctors
in Noah's garden, but they
don't bring him Jessica.

Noah is fighting with pirates again.
Noisy pirates.

They rumble and tumble
and swish swords of steel.

"Ahhhhh-haaaa!" yells Noah.
He scares them away—for now.

Pirates hide sneakily
in Noah's garden.

Noah is spying on
helicopters again.
Huge helicopters.

They thunder and boom
as they blast through the air.

"Oh, wow!" breathes Noah.
They hover above, then land.

Helicopters come quickly
in Noah's garden.

"Will Jessica ever see my garden?"

"Maybe one day," says Dad, closing his eyes.

"Perhaps she will," says Mom, "if you wish for her."

Noah smiles.

Wishes are made in Noah's garden.
He will make one for Jessica.

Noah is wishing with Grandad again.

At the fountain.

He aims and he throws

and announces his wish.

"For Jessica," says Noah.

The coin soars upward, then plops.

Grandad smiles gently in Noah's garden.

"Is there a boy named Noah
in this garden?" asks Dad.

"Yes!" Noah says. "I'm here."

"Cover your eyes," says Mom.

Surprises come suddenly in Noah's garden.

And this surprise is . . .

Jessica!

For Theresa
M. J.

For Sasha, Louise, and Mia, who can
turn a garden shed into a castle
A. J.

First U.S. edition 2010

Library of Congress Cataloging-in-Publication Data

Johnson, Mo.
Noah's garden : when someone you love is in the hospital /
Mo Johnson ; illustrated by Annabelle Josse. —1st U.S. ed.
p. cm.
Summary: In a garden near a hospital, young Noah has imaginary
adventures while waiting anxiously with his family for his new baby
sister, who has a serious medical condition, to be released.
ISBN 978-0-7636-4782-7
[1. Brothers and sisters—Fiction. 2. Sick—Fiction.
3. Babies—Fiction. 4. Hospitals—Fiction.
5. Gardens—Fiction.] I. Josse, Annabelle, ill. II. Title.
PZ7.J634165No 2010
[E]—dc22   2009046544

10 11 12 13 14 15 16 SCP
1 2 3 4 5 6 7 8 9 10

Printed in Humen, Dongguan, China

This book was typeset in Godlike Emboldened and Tree Boxelder.
The illustrations were done in watercolor.

Candlewick Press
99 Dover Street
Somerville, Massachusetts 02144

visit us at www.candlewick.com

On December 6, 2005, Jessica Titmus was
born at the Royal Children's Hospital in
Melbourne, Australia, with hypoplastic
left heart syndrome (HLHS). The story of
her successful fight for life can be accessed
through Hearts of Hope, Australia.

During her seven-month stay, Jessica,
her parents, Paul and Elese, and her
brother, Noah, showed great courage
and resilience in the face of adversity.
Noah's Garden pays tribute to this special
family and to the skill of the staff at RCH
Melbourne, Australia, and beyond. It also
recognizes the importance of hospital
gardens and the people who tend them.